D1110994

THE MYSTERY IN THE Smoky Mountains

First Edition

Published by Gallopade International/Carole Marsh Books. Printed in the United States of America.

Editor: Janice Baker
Assistant Editor: Paige Muh
Cover Design: Vicki DeJoy
Content Design: Randolyn Friedlander

Gallopade International is introducing SAT words that kids need to know in each new book that we publish. The SAT words are bold in the story. Look for this special logo beside each word in the glossary. Happy Learning!

Gallopade is proud to be a member and supporter of these educational organizations and associations:

American Booksellers Association
American Library Association
International Reading Association
National Association for Gifted Children
The National School Supply and Equipment Association
The National Council for the Social Studies
Museum Store Association
Association of Partners for Public Lands
Association of Booksellers for Children
Association for the Study of African American Life and History
National Alliance of Black School Educators

Once upon a time...

Papa said ...
Why don't you set the stories in real locations?
Mystery Girl
That's a great idea! And if I do that, I might as well choose real kids as characters in the stories! But which kids would I pick?
MiMi, PiCK ME, PiCK ME!
ME, TOO, MiMi, PiCK ME, TOO!
Christina
Grant

You two really are characters, that's all I've got to say!

Yes you are! And, of course I choose you! But what should I write about?

National Parks!

Famous Places!

FUN PLACES!

Disney World!

New York City!

Dracula's Castle

On the *Mystery Girl* airplane ...

I CAN FLY US ANYWHERE!

Or aboard the *Mimi*!

Or by surfboard, rickshaw, motorbike, camel ...

All great ideas! I can put a lot of history, MYSTERY, legend, lore, and laughs in the books! We can use other boys and girls in the books. It will be educational and fun!

And can you put some cool stuff online? Like a Book Club and a Scavenger Hunt and a Map so we can track our adventures?

And so, Mimi, Papa, Christina, and Grant took off aboard the *Mystery Girl* and America's National Mystery Book Series—where the adventure is real and so are the characters! —was born.

START YOUR ADVENTURE TODAY!

1
FOLKLORE GALORE!

Christina looked up from her book and gazed out the airplane window. She felt the *Mystery Girl's* nose turn down for initial descent into the airport. It had been a short flight in the little airplane. It felt like they had just taken off!

"Gosh, Papa! That was fast!" Christina said to the pilot in a black cowboy hat, who also happened to be her grandfather.

"Uh, can you make it faster, please, Papa?" pleaded Grant, Christina's little brother. "I gotta go! Say, when are you gonna get a bathroom on this plane?"

Mimi giggled at her grandson squirming in his seat, his face twisted in discomfort. "Grant, I told you not to drink that sports drink before we left!" she said. She shut her shiny silver laptop computer and stuffed her red, sparkly mystery-writing glasses into her purse.

Mimi and Papa often brought their grandchildren, Christina and Grant, on research trips. Mimi wrote children's mystery books, and trips with her cowboy-pilot husband and her adventure-seeking grandkids were the best part of her job! This morning they traveled from Peachtree City, Georgia to Asheville, North Carolina, for Mimi to research folklore of the Great Smoky Mountains.

Christina yanked her long, brown hair into a quick ponytail and gazed out the window again. Mountains reached up to the clouds as far as she could see. Not the jagged, dark, rocky kind, but, rolling, tree-covered hills that stretched lazily toward the horizon. The autumn leaves on the trees created a collage of colors on the mountains–fiery orange, brick red, chestnut brown, and saffron yellow. Out of the corner of her eye, she spotted a plume of blue-grey smoke rising from the valleys between the mountain peaks.

"Grant, we'll stop at a bathroom as soon as we get to the airport, but you'll have to make it snappy!" said Papa. "We still have an hour drive to Penland School and we've got to get there by lunchtime."

"Wait, why are we going to a school?" asked Grant, shifting from side to side. "We're on fall break from our school. Why do we have to go to another one?"

"It's Penland School for Crafts, Grant," said Mimi. "Students of all ages come there to learn to make crafts and other beautiful works of art. It's the perfect place to start our travels through the Smoky Mountains."

"Well, as long as they're serving lunch, I'll go! I'm starved," said Grant.

"Typical!" said Christina. She leaned over to her brother and tousled his curly, blond hair.

The moment they landed at the Asheville airport and pulled into the hangar, Grant sprinted toward the nearest bathroom.

Once he rejoined the group, the four travelers hopped into their rental car and Papa steered them toward Skyline Drive and the scenic trip north through Asheville.

In the back seat, Christina's stomach growled. She was so excited about the trip that morning, she didn't eat breakfast. She picked up her backpack and sifted through the contents. Maybe there's a leftover granola bar from school last week, she thought.

"Christina, grab your camera," said Mimi. "You'll want to take pictures of the scenery as we head through Asheville and up into the mountains. We've picked the best time of year to visit the Great Smokies!"

"We sure have," said Papa. "I love the canopy of autumn leaves and smell of the brisk fall air in these mountains!"

Instead of food, Christina pulled her camera from her backpack and began snapping pictures of the natural mountain beauty. Houses dotted the landscape, nestled within the trees and hills. Sometimes, faraway views peeked through the gorges that separated each mountaintop. Again she noticed wisps of white and blue-tinted smoke whirling up from the mountains.

The SUV circled up and around the side of a mountain, passing a slower car on the right. Suddenly, Grant's ears felt like they had filled with water. He felt pressure inside his head.

"Everything sounds weird in my head!" he yelped.

"It's OK, Grant!" said Christina. "Your ears are adjusting to the altitude of the mountains. Papa always says to swallow really hard and that will fix it."

Grant took a big gulp and the feeling in his ears returned to normal. Mimi and Papa gave each other a knowing glance. They were happy that their grandchildren actually remembered some of the helpful advice they had shared over the years!

"Kids, these mountains are filled with history and legend and folklore–galore!" said Mimi, adjusting the red ribbon on her wide-brimmed straw hat. "You only see orange and brown leaves and rocks and cliffs from the car, but when we visit the places I have planned for us, you'll be amazed at what you'll find! They don't call these the GREAT Smoky Mountains for nothing!"

Christina was about to ask Mimi if the smoke she saw rising from the mountains was the reason they were called the "Smoky Mountains," but Papa announced that they were almost at Penland School. That question would save for later.

Christina's stomach rumbled again. She caught Grant's attention and rubbed her belly. She wanted her brother to know that she was ready for lunch as much as he was! If only she had known what mysterious adventure would begin that day, she would have been sure to eat a healthy breakfast before she left home!

2

A PART OF A SECTION OF A WHOLE!

As Papa drove up the winding road to the school, Grant studied a map intently. Christina knew he was thinking hard because his tongue was sticking out of the side of his mouth and his face looked serious. Shaking the map in the air, Grant spoke. "Hey, what's going on here?" he said. "This map is trying to trick me. It says we're in three places at the same time!"

"Hmmm," said Mimi, turning to look at her grandson in the back seat. "That sounds like a mystery we need to solve!"

Grant handed Mimi his map. "See right here," he said, pointing to some gray triangles. "It says we are in the Appalachian Mountains

AND the Blue Ridge Mountains *AND* the Great Smoky Mountains."

Papa pointed his index finger into the air. "This is no mystery, my boy," he said. "We are traveling right in the middle of a *part* of a *section* of a *whole*!"

Grant threw his hands on top of his head and shook it back and forth. "OK, now my head's going to explode!" he said. "A *what* of a *who* of a *how*?"

Papa explained, "The Appalachian Mountains are a *whole* mountain range, running from Alabama north to Canada. The Blue Ridge Mountains are a *section* of the Appalachian range, the eastern edge of the range, actually. The Great Smoky Mountains are *part* of the Blue Ridge Mountains. Specifically, they are the mountains along the North Carolina and Tennessee border."

It took a minute, but Grant's face lit up with understanding.

"Now I get it!" he declared. "It's just like eating pizza. I have a whole pizza. I take one section–that's the slice. Then I eat the anchovies first. The anchovies are a part of a section of a whole!"

"Ewwwww! Anchovies!" squealed Christina in disgust. How could her brother eat something so gross? No matter how hungry she was, she could NEVER eat anchovies!

Grant leaned over to his sister and licked his lips! "Mmmm mmmm good!!" he teased.

Trying to erase her annoying brother and oily fish parts from her mind, Christina peered out of the car window at the mountains in the distance. They looked like waves on the ocean, only with tints of orange and red instead of green and blue. More wisps of smoke caught her eye–lighter wisps this time.

"I guess the Smoky Mountains are named for all the smoke I've seen here," said Christina.

"Are the mountains on fire?" asked Grant. "Should we call the fire department, Papa?"

"No, my boy, it's not that kind of smoke," said Papa, pulling the car into a parking space. "It's actually a kind of mist.

The warm air from the base of the mountains mixes with the cool air along the top of the mountains. That creates the smoke you see."

It was a perfectly beautiful day with a clear, blue sky, but the smoke added an eerie and mysterious feel to an otherwise **tranquil** setting. Smoke, mist, fog–whatever you call it–I don't want to be in those mountains by myself, thought Christina.

3
CRAZY CRAFTING CARTER

Penland School of Crafts wasn't like any school Christina and Grant had ever seen. Several rustic log and brick buildings nestled among the oak and fir trees, rhododendron bushes, and grassy fields. The rolling mountains in their autumn finery loomed behind the entire school. Adults were all over the place, but no one seemed to be in a hurry to get to class. They sat in rocking chairs on porches, ate on picnic benches under trees, or milled around building entrances.

"Are all these people teachers?" asked Grant. He noticed there wasn't a single kid in sight.

"You have to be at least 18 to go to school here, Grant," said Mimi. "These folks study the art of making all kinds of crafts–papermaking, metalworks, clay, glassblowing, textiles, painting, photography..." Mimi's voice trailed off, lost in her love of all things crafty.

"All I know is that if I went to school here, I'd NEVER come inside!" said Grant. "Look at all the trees I'd climb and the places I would explore!"

Grant was right. Penland's campus was tucked into a mountain setting as pretty as a postcard. The trees, hills, and **vales** stretched on forever!

"Let's head to the Craft House gallery," said Papa. "We're supposed to meet Carter there."

Carter Morgan was an artsy friend of Mimi and Papa, who they knew when they lived in Tryon, North Carolina. He taught glassblowing classes at Penland. When he heard Mimi and Papa were coming to the Smoky Mountains on a research trip, he invited them to visit the school.

"Wow," said Christina, following her grandparents into one of the school's craft galleries. Intricate wooden figurines, colorful glassblown bottles, huge steel carvings, and unusual furniture crowded every surface.

Grant found a display of porcelain bowls with tiny birds perched on the edge. His hand reached up to touch one.

"You break, you buy, young'un!" said a man's deep voice. "And I'll bet that bowl costs more than your allowance!"

Grant's hand quickly dropped to his side. He turned to see a man about Papa's age. The snowy white hair on the man's head stuck out every-which-way. A paintbrush rested behind one ear with a small gold earring in it. His brown pants were wrinkled and smudged with dirt, and the laces of his hiking boots weren't even tied. He was grinning from ear to ear at Grant.

"Good to see you, Carter!" said Papa, shaking the man's hand. "What a place this is!"

"This school is a treasure in these Smoky Mountains," said Carter, running his fingers through his hair. "People from all walks of life and from all over the world come here to study and learn about the art of making crafts."

"Each piece is extraordinary and unique," said Mimi, admiring a painting through her sparkly glasses.

"Not only are these crafts art," Carter continued, "the process of *making* these crafts is an art. It's a tradition handed down for years and years."

"I know people here make crafts," said Grant. "But does anyone here make sandwiches?"

"I've got hungry grandchildren, Carter!" said Papa. "How about a little Western North Carolina barbeque and some sweet tea?"

Carter slapped his knee and laughed heartily. "Alrighty then, young'uns!" he exclaimed. "Let's wet our whistles and fill our gullets! Follow me!"

Grant didn't know what to think of Carter Morgan. He didn't look like or talk like any of his grandparents' other friends. He shrugged his shoulders and happily trailed Carter to the dining hall. Any friend who filled his gullet with lunch was OK by him!

4
BELIEVE IT, OR NOT!

When they weren't eating, laughing, or telling stories, the adults talked about the research Mimi was doing for her new books. She explained her love of Appalachian folklore and history. The lifestyles, traditions, and legends of people who lived in the Smoky Mountains for generations interested her the most.

Mimi ticked off a list. "The quilts, the pottery, the food, the music, the clothes, the architecture, the games, the language, the stories–you name it! I love it ALL!" she said.

"We're driving through Cherokee this afternoon," said Papa, referring to the town named after one of the original Native

American tribes who inhabited the area. "The Cherokee legends are wonderful stories!"

Grant slurped up the last bit of sweet tea from his glass. "Mimi, what makes a legend different from a regular story?" he asked.

"Ahhh, Grant. Good question," replied Mimi. "A legend is a story that has been told and retold for a long, long time–even passed down from generation to generation. The story is so old that it is believed to be true, but no one can actually prove it."

"If you can't prove it, how do you know if a legend is true?" asked Grant.

"The mystery is that you may *never really* know for sure," said Mimi, a twinkle in her eyes.

"Ain't that the truth!" said Carter with another hearty laugh. "Do you young'uns wanna hear my favorite Cherokee legend?"

"Sure!" the kids chimed.

"There is an enchanted waterfall in the Great Smoky Mountains," began Carter. He leaned close to Grant and Christina, his voice a low whisper, as if he didn't want anyone else to hear. "This waterfall empties into a lake that's hidden underneath the hemlock trees and the rhododendron thickets at the base of the Smokies' highest mountain. Bears, hawks, salamanders, raccoons, elk, and all the wildlife of the mountains gather at this lake in autumn. They believe its water heals wounded animals and fortifies them for the harsh mountain winters. But no human has ever seen this lake. The Cherokee say that only a person who is pure of heart and causes no harm to even the smallest mountain animal can find this lake."

"Uh, that sounds like a *not-true* legend, if you ask me," said Grant matter-of-factly.

"Oh, Grant, don't be so quick to disbelieve," cautioned the old man. "Some say they've seen black bears and red foxes, wild turkeys and tree frogs walking side by side into the trees toward the sound of falling water."

Christina looked outside at the peaceful landscape. Earlier, the mountain smoke gave her an eerie feeling. Now this story of magical waterfalls and wild animals gave her the heebee-jeebies! Maybe some fresh mountain air would make her feel better, she thought.

The kids gobbled up the rest of their lunches and wandered outside to explore. Small gusts of wind blew through the tree branches as orange and red leaves drifted to the ground. Christina sifted through the pile of leaves to find the most beautiful colors and shapes.

Grant found a birch tree with branches low enough to climb. He hoisted himself into the tree and then shimmied halfway up. He was shocked when he realized he wasn't the only climber in that tree!

5
FALLING FRIEND

A loud CRACK of a snapping branch startled Christina! Suddenly, four arms, four legs, two heads, and hundreds of leaves tumbled out of the tree and hit the ground with a THUD!

"OUCH!" exclaimed Grant. He groaned at first and then giggled. Orange and brown leaves stuck out of his curly hair and the broken tree limb lay near his feet.

Christina was surprised to see her brother drop out of a tree. She was even more surprised to see a girl on the ground next to him! "Are you OK?" she asked the two former tree climbers.

The girl's long, reddish-brown hair was decorated with leaves just like Grant's. She adjusted the small wire-framed glasses on her nose and jumped up. "Happens all the time," she said, brushing off her denim overalls. "Y'all must be Christina and Grant. I'm Elizabeth Morgan. My grandfather said you were coming here with your grandparents today. I'm excited to meet you because I love your grandmother's mystery books!"

"Do you live here with your grandfather?" asked Christina.

"I visit him for a week every autumn. I help him with his glassblowing workshops in the mornings and explore the mountains in the afternoons."

"You're lucky," said Grant. "These mountains are awesome! But these trees are a little dangerous!" He examined a tear in his brand-new jeans.

"Cowboys and cowgirls! Round 'em up!" bellowed Papa from a nearby porch.

The kids scampered over to the adults. Papa had his cowboy hat on his head and Mimi had her purse, signaling that it was time to go!

"Glad you kids have met because we're going to be spending more time together," said Papa. "Carter has to give tours of the school over the next two days, so Elizabeth is joining us on our trip!"

"The more the merrier," chimed Mimi happily. "Appalachia, here we come!"

While the others climbed in the car, Grant ran back into the Craft House for one more bathroom stop before the ride to Cherokee.

When he returned to the car, he leaned over to his sister. "Uh, Christina," he whispered. "You'll never believe what I just found."

He opened his hand to reveal a surprise. This trip was going to be mysterious after all!

6

A BLUE CLUE IN A BLUE RIDGE!

For the journey to Cherokee, Papa turned the SUV south onto the Blue Ridge Parkway. "Got some magnificent scenery ahead," he announced.

The Blue Ridge Parkway was a two-lane road winding its way through the Appalachian Mountains from Virginia down through the Smokies. Spectacular views surrounded it, as if the road wanted its drivers to notice every inch of the mountains' natural beauty. Rocky cliffs dropped into orange and gold tree-covered valleys. Small waterfalls trickled into streams. Split rail fences criss-crossed along the roadside. Meadows of grass glowed yellow in anticipation of winter. Rustic, wooden houses and barns stood along the mountain side–some vacant and dilapidated, some hearty and still in use.

Grant rolled down his window and stuck his head partially out. Cool autumn air tickled his face. Papa tuned the radio to some station playing banjo music. Since when did his grandfather listen to banjo music, Grant wondered.

Every few miles revealed a roadside overlook where cars full of sightseers could pull over to enjoy the view. After two miles of begging, the kids convinced Papa to alter his travel schedule and pull over at a roadside stop. While Mimi and Papa read a sign about Appalachian plant life, Christina, Grant and Elizabeth wandered over to railing. They wanted to admire the mountain **vistas** and to discuss what Grant found at Penland.

"So what do you think this is all about?" asked Grant. He yanked the mysterious item from his jeans pocket. It was a piece of heavy, fibrous, blue paper folded into a small square. "That's paper they make in papermaking workshops at my grandfather's school," said Elizabeth.

"Well, it was laying on the floor outside the bathroom," said Grant. "Almost like someone wanted me to find it."

Christina unfolded the paper and read:

Near a native from
times of old,
a mountain
legend will unfold

"What do you think that means?" asked Elizabeth, taking the paper and analyzing it for herself.

"Someone wants us to learn about a legend," said Christina. "A mountain legend–maybe like the one Carter told us earlier."

"Are you talking about the legend of the enchanted waterfall?" asked Elizabeth. "That's his favorite!"

"Why wouldn't someone just tell us about a legend?" wondered Grant.

Christina remembered the creepy feeling she had earlier. "Legends can be mysterious," she said. "Maybe it is a legend we have to keep secret."

Grant picked up tiny rocks and dropped them over the railing. It was fun to see a rock skip and tumble down the side of the mountain until it was out of sight. "So where do we find an old-timey native?" he asked, referring to the clue. "I'll bet there's one in those old-timey, broken-down barns we just passed!"

Christina shrugged her shoulders. "I don't know exactly where we can find a native," she said. "Considering how you got this clue, I bet the native will find us!" But did they really want him to?

7
SCULPTED SEQUOYAH

At the southern end of the Blue Ridge Parkway was the town of Cherokee, considered the gateway to the Smoky Mountains. Mimi shared the significance of Cherokee as they drove into town.

"This town is a living history lesson about the Cherokee people," she said. "Museums, theaters, and stores display artifacts and tell stories of how the Cherokee inhabited the Smoky Mountains for thousands of years. Then white settlers from Europe came in the 1700s and 1800s and pushed the Cherokee out of their native land. Some Cherokee people returned to the Smoky

Mountains over time and they lived to tell the history of their tribe."

Grant noticed signs as they drove through town–authentic Native American places like Oconaluftee, Qualla, and Bearmeats. "Bearmeats?" he exclaimed. "I hope no bear meets me!"

Arriving at the Cherokee Indian Museum, Mimi hunted for a statue of Sequoyah, the Native American who invented the Cherokee alphabet in the early 1800s. It didn't take them long to find it.

A wooden statue of Sequoyah dominated a small courtyard at the front of the museum. It was as tall as the museum building itself and probably 20 people could sit on the stone bench encircling its base.

"That is one GIGANTIC Native American!" said Grant. "That reminds me of a joke. Hey Christina, did Native Americans hunt bear?"

"I don't know," said Christina, waiting for the punchline.

"Well," Grant said, "certainly not in winter!"

While Grant rolled with laughter at his own joke, Christina and Elizabeth just groaned.

Christina gazed up at the angular carving of Sequoyah. Deep markings lined his face and something resembling a head scarf and feather perched on top of his head. She noticed something that startled her–the wooden tears coming from Sequoyah's eyes.

"Why is he crying?" Christina asked Papa.

"The tears signify the pain caused when the settlers forced the Cherokee to leave their land," said Papa. "The Cherokee walked west on what is now known as the 'Trail of Tears.' All suffered terribly and many, many died."

"So sad," said Elizabeth. "How painful it must have been to leave their homes and these gorgeous mountains."

Christina ran her hands along Sequoyah's nooks and crannies, feeling the smooth wood beneath her fingers. Suddenly, she felt a soft, thin object give way near the base of the sculpture. She stopped and peered at what she touched. It was a piece of rolled leather, tied with a piece a twine. Christina gently pulled it from its hiding spot. She raced over to Grant and Elizabeth who were playing leap frog in the grass.

"Hey! Look!" she called. "Remember how I said that the old-timey native would find us? Well, I think he just did!"

8

GRANT'S NATIVE TONGUE?

"How did Sequoyah hand you that piece of cloth?" Grant asked. He glanced from his sister to the wooden statue and back to his sister. "He doesn't have hands!"

Christina slapped her forehead with her palm. Her brother drove her nuts sometimes! "Grant! Of course he didn't hand it to me!" she griped. "It's a wooden statue! I just found it tucked into one of the gaps in the wood."

The twine untied easily and Christina unrolled the leather. Grant and Elizabeth crowded around her to get a closer look.

Letters were scratched into the leather's surface. No matter how hard she tried, Christina couldn't understand what they meant.

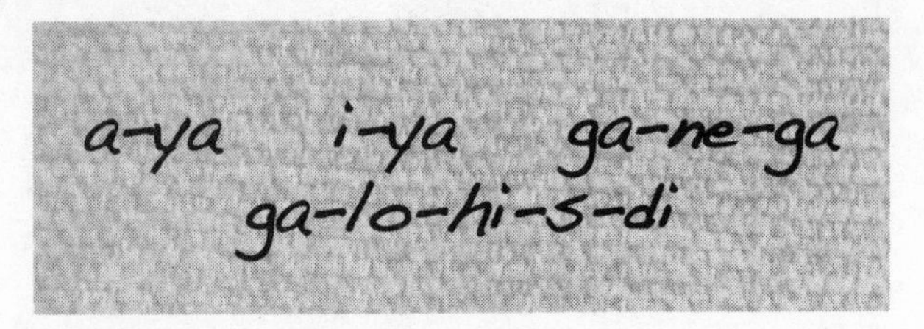

"Are those even words?" Elizabeth asked. "What's with all the dashes?"

"Let me see that," said Grant, snatching the leather from Christina's hand. He studied the words from all angles. His finger tapped the top of his head while he thought.

"Aww, this is easy!" he concluded. "It's written in Cherokee. I'll translate it for you." Christina and Elizabeth looked at him like he had two heads.

"Grant, has this mountain air made you batty?" Christina asked. "You can't read Cherokee!" Her brother might know a little Spanish and even some pig Latin–but these Cherokee words were another story!

"Maybe not, but I know someone who can help us," replied Grant.

"Who?" asked Elizabeth.

"Well, Sequoyah, of course!" Grant explained. "Check this out! Mimi said Sequoyah invented the Cherokee alphabet, right?"

"Umm, right," answered Christina.

"On the bench over there, I found a piece of paper showing Sequoyah's Cherokee alphabet," said Grant. "It also lists some Cherokee words with their English meanings."

"Way to go, Grant!" said Christina. "Let's see if we can find these words and translate the clue."

Grant slid his finger from word to word until he found the ones he was looking for.

"*A-ya*...frosted. *I-ya*...pumpkin. *Ga-ne-ga*...hides. *Ga-lo-hi-s-di*...way?" said Grant. "Frosted pumpkin hides the way?"

"Can that be right?" asked Christina. "That doesn't make any sense. What's a frosted pumpkin?"

Always thinking about food, Grant suggested, "Pumpkin pie with whipped cream frosting, maybe?"

"I doubt it, little brother," replied Christina. "I sure wish Sequoyah could tell us what this means." She glanced at the statue, wishing he would suddenly spring to life and answer their questions.

Talk of pumpkin pie triggered Grant's appetite. "Snack time!" he announced, sauntering off to tell Mimi.

Because it was late in the afternoon, Mimi squashed his hopes for food.

"You'll ruin your supper," she said. "We're going to dinner at Peg and Wilbur's and they live right up the road. You can have all you can eat when we get there."

Grant's face turned from disappointment to joy when he heard his favorite words! "Ni-ga-da ni-hi hi-'gi!" he said. Now he could say "all you can eat" in English, Spanish, French, and Cherokee!

Mimi and Papa froze in their tracks, stunned to hear their grandson speaking fluent Cherokee. Flabbergasted, Mimi asked, "Grant, since when have you learned to speak Cherokee?"

Grant grinned mischievously, thinking about the Cherokee word list that was now folded in his back pocket. “Aww, Mimi,” teased Grant, “that’ll just have to be a mystery, won’t it?”

Christina stuffed Sequoyah’s leather clue in her backpack. Her mind overflowed with questions. Cherokee words, hidden clues, a mountain legend, and a frosted pumpkin, she thought. Where were these clues leading them?

9
LOG CABIN LIVING

"Who are Peg and Wilbur and what are they serving for dinner?" Grant asked Mimi and Papa.

Papa cautioned his grandson. "No matter what they are serving for supper, you will eat and be grateful," he said. He expected mannerly behavior from Christina and Grant–no exceptions!

"Peg and Wilbur Walker own the Mumble Peg Bookstore just north of Bryson City," explained Mimi. "They've sold my books for a long, long time and we've been friends for even longer!"

Grant snickered. "Mountain pigs should talk more clearly!" he joked. "It's hard to understand a pig that mumbles!"

"Mumble PEG–not pig!" corrected Papa. "Mumble Peg is an old-timey game kids play tossing pocketknives!"

"Tossing pocketknives?" asked Christina, surprised. "Mom barely lets us use a butter knife to put peanut butter on crackers! I can't believe kids up here are allowed to play with pocketknives!"

"Mountain life is much different than city life," Mimi said. "That's why I love it! Even though we're in the 21st century, folks up here continue the same traditions and lifestyles they've had for more than a century. It's so important to preserve that heritage and share it with future generations!"

A short drive through the tree-covered mountains dropped Christina, Grant and Elizabeth smack in the middle of the old-timey lifestyle Mimi loved!

Peg and Wilbur Walker's driveway was a dirt road that led to a charming mountain cove. A stream ran alongside the dirt road, its bubbling water tumbling over mossy rocks on its way down the mountainside. The setting sun cast an orange glow over the entire landscape, creating a warm, welcoming atmosphere, even on a cool autumn evening.

The Walkers lived in the large-framed log cabin that rested at the foot of the nearby mountain. Its outside walls were weathered and worn, like some of the abandoned houses they passed on the Blue Ridge Parkway. At each corner of the cabin, notches in the wood locked the round logs together. Smoke curled from the top of a stacked stone chimney. Grant noticed a small rectangular opening cut into the wood right next to the chimney. That's a weird place to have a window, he thought.

"I built a house just like this with those Lincoln Logs Papa gave me," Grant said. Not a fan of video games, Papa always encouraged Grant to play with the toys he loved as a child. Rocking chairs and a bench swing sat empty on the front porch. Wind chimes jangled in the breeze. On the front steps, an old hound dog jumped to attention, barking and howling to alert his owners that someone had arrived.

Peg and Wilbur appeared on the front porch to welcome their guests.

"Welcome to our holler!" bellowed Wilbur, in his Appalachian twang. "We're shore glad you'uns have come to see us!" The tall, lanky man, dressed in denim and flannel, kissed Mimi on the cheek and slapped Papa on the back. He grabbed three suitcases from the car and carried them into the cabin.

Peg hugged every kid as if she'd known them for years. She had an apron tied around her waist and her hair was pinned back into a neat bun. "Y'all gotta be hungry, I reckon!" she said. "I've been fixin' supper for you. C'mon in!"

Grant, Christina, and Elizabeth cautiously followed the adults into the cabin, unsure of what they would find inside. "I feel like we have time traveled back to pioneer days or something," Christina whispered to her brother.

Inside, the kids found one spacious room that served as a living room, dining room and kitchen. Each area of the room had its own furniture–sofas, tables, oil lamps, cupboards, and old kitchen appliances. A fire crackled in the stone fireplace. Steep wooden steps ascended to an open, airy loft.

The log cabin that had looked stark and cold from the outside was warm and cozy inside. Peg and Wilbur's guests felt right at home.

Grant immediately noticed the Walker's home didn't have a TV set. "You don't have a TV?" he asked Wilbur.

"Naw!" Wilbur replied. "We don't. There're better things to do 'round here than watch TV! You'll see!"

Grant wondered if that had anything to do with playing with pocketknives, but he didn't ask. Instead, he decided to wash his hands before dinner. "Could you please show me where the bathroom is?" Grant asked Wilbur politely.

"Aww, sonny," said Wilbur, "we don't have one of those either!"

10
OUTHOUSE ORDEAL

The silverware in Christina's hand clanked to the floor when she heard Wilbur say there was no bathroom in the cabin. Even Mimi stopped her conversation with Peg and looked at Papa with concern.

"Whadaya mean, no bathroom?" asked Grant.

"We've got an outhouse out yonder," replied Wilbur, pointing out the window at the back of the cabin. "It's got a lantern and a Sears catalog you can use to clean up."

Grant tried to make sense of Wilbur's words. "Are you saying we have to go outside in the dark to an old timey port-o-potty and then use pages of a catalog to...to...wipe?" Grant asked, barely whispering the last word.

Wilbur's laughter roared to the rafters. He loved it when city folk experienced life in their home. The mountains forced people to slow down and appreciate the scenery...and the outhouses!

Christina was horrified. She looked at her grandparents, her eyes pleading for a ride to the nearest motel. But ever the optimist, Mimi corralled the kids outside for a visit to the Walker's outhouse. "It'll be fine," she said, reassuring the kids (and herself)!

The sky was dark and clouds floated past the full moon, making things even blacker. Chirping crickets and the babbling stream combined for spooky background music. An owl called a low *hoo-hoo* from the barn in the meadow. Christina wondered what was worse: being out in the dark in the middle of nowhere or using the outhouse.

The outdoor bathroom looked like a miniature log cabin, but was painted white. Wilbur said white was easier to see in the dark. Over the door, a crescent moon shape was carved out of the wood.

From behind the outhouse, two masked furballs suddenly raced straight at Grant. He screamed and jumped on Christina's back for a piggy-back ride rescue. "Yikes! We're being attacked by outhouse bandits!" he cried.

"Calm down, Grant!" Christina told her brother, shaking him off her back. "Those bandits are raccoons. And they're probably just out looking for food."

"They're so cute," said Elizabeth. "I think the animals are my favorite part of visiting the mountains! My granddad told me that there are thousands of animal species around here."

"Mimi, I've got an outhouse joke for you," said Grant, trying to make the best of their situation. "If you're American when you go into an outhouse, and you're American when you come out of an outhouse, what are you when you're INSIDE an outhouse?"

Mimi waited for the answer to her grandson's latest potty joke. "I don't know," she said.

"Eur-o-pean!" cried Grant. "Get it???"

"Oh, Grant!" said Mimi, putting her hand over her mouth to hide her smile. She acted like she didn't approve of his joke, but finally she laughed out loud. She really was always a kid at heart!

When Grant's giggles ended, he took a deep breath and held it, his cheeks puffed out on each side. Then he swung open the outhouse door and disappeared inside.

"What a relief!" he called, his voice echoing in the still air. "There's toilet paper in here. Now I can read the catalog instead of use it!"

Only a boy could find something good about using an outhouse, thought Christina. She was ready to go back to the cozy cabin. Clouds now hid the moon completely and it was getting colder. A chill slithered up her spine. The Walkers' land was beautiful in the daytime but pretty creepy at night!

11
CORNPONE CORNPONE!

Peg's dinner took the kids' minds off their trip to the outhouse. Everyone's mouth watered at the delectable sights and smells spread from one end of the knotty pine table to the other.

"You know, it's really great that you recycle," said Grant, looking around the table. "My teacher says recycling is very important to the environment."

Christina glanced at Elizabeth and mouthed the word "What?" Elizabeth shrugged her shoulders.

Papa looked around the room trying to understand what his grandson was talking about. "Boy, what in the name of sassafras tea are you talking about?" he asked.

"Well, we're all drinking from old jars," he said, holding up his mason jar filled with sweet tea. "Looks like they eat lots of jelly and then keep the jars to drink out of!"

"We got a lot a teachin' to do about mountain life," said Wilbur, patting Grant on the back. "You'uns are city folk through and through!"

"Eat up," said Peg, passing bowls and platters down the table. It was a Smoky Mountain feast and Grant was in heaven.

Peg offered up each of her dishes. "We've got mountain trout, beef stew, squash burgers, deviled eggs, green beans, pickle relish, sweet potato biscuits, and cornpone."

Grant grabbed a hunk of cornbread from the cast iron skillet and quietly chanted, "Cornpone cornpone greasy greasy! Coats my belly easy easy!" He hadn't realized everyone heard him until he looked up from his plate and saw all eyes staring his way. His face turned fresh-from-the-vine tomato red.

"We chant that on the playground sometimes!" he said taking a huge bite. "I didn't even know what cornpone was until now! But I'm sure glad it's coating my belly tonight!" A smear of gooey butter greased his chin.

Although everyone was stuffed, they made room for dessert–Peg's famous strawberry rhubarb pie topped with vanilla ice cream! "Ohhhhh," said Papa, patting his stomach. "I don't need to eat for a week after this feast!"

After a few card games, the kids were ready for bed. Peg and Wilbur graciously gave the loft and its two beds to their guests. Christina, Elizabeth, and Grant scurried up the steps to turn in for the night. Now was their chance to talk about the clue they found in Cherokee that afternoon.

"We're looking for a frosted pumpkin," said Christina. "Whatever that is."

"You know, I saw some pumpkins in the front yard," said Elizabeth. "The dog was lying next to them!"

"Were they covered in frosting?" asked Grant. He still hoped this clue had something to do with dessert!

"No frosting," admitted Elizabeth.

"I wonder who would be leaving us these clues anyway?" asked Christina. "And more importantly, what legend is so secret that we need clues to learn about it? This is so strange!"

Elizabeth and Christina nestled down into a cushy, cozy feather bed. Matching squares of calico cloth decorated the counterpane quilt covering the bed. It looked like a fabric checkerboard. The girls snuggled under its comforting colors.

Saving the other bed for Mimi and Papa, Grant wrapped up in his own quilt on the floor. Too tired to talk about clues and legends anymore, they each drifted off to sleep. They slept soundly, until the most unexpected, ear-splitting noises jolted them from their dreams!

12
SHIVAREE TIMBERS!

BANG! The noise scared Elizabeth so much that she fell out of bed and landed on the floor! Grant jumped up so fast he knocked his head on the loft railing. Christina's legs tangled in the quilt as she tried to escape the bed and see what all the commotion was about.

"What's happening?" cried Christina, trapped in the covers. Grant and Elizabeth could barely hear her voice over the deafening noise coming from downstairs.

Rubbing the goose egg on his head caused by the railing, Grant peered over the side of the loft. "It looks like...well, a parade!" he replied.

Twenty of Peg and Wilbur's mountain neighbors marched around the cabin, each creating their own thunderous rhythm. Banging pots and pans, clanking sticks and cans, clanging bells, shrill whistles, and squeaky fiddles rattled the family pictures perched precariously on the walls. Masks concealed some of the musicians' faces, while others wore colorful hats and scarves. All of them whooped and hollered, not caring that they had just scared the daylights out of three sleeping kids. Even Mimi and Papa howled with laughter at the show.

The kids scrambled down the stairs and joined Mimi and Papa in the center of the festivities. The banging and clanging died down and frantic fiddle music took its place. Soon Peg, Wilbur, Mimi, Papa, and everyone else in the cabin was dancing.

The music was lively and fast. The fiddler ran the bow back and forth across the strings so quickly Christina's eyes couldn't follow it. She and Elizabeth moved outside the group and clapped to the rhythm of the music, a little too shy to boogie with the others.

In the center of the crowd and still dressed in Spiderman pajamas, Grant appeared! He leaped and clopped and shimmied, keeping time with the furious fiddle. Then he locked arms and do-si-doed with a little old lady in a red plaid housedress, who looked thrilled to be dancing with such a nice, young, city boy!

The fiddler played and played, moving from one song to the next without stopping. Grant finally grabbed Christina and Elizabeth and swung them around the dusty pine floor along with him. All three danced until they finally collapsed on the floor in a pile of sweaty giggles.

Eventually, the music ended and the rowdy group left the cabin more quietly than they arrived. The fiddle player was the last to leave. With a wink, he handed his bow to Grant as he stepped into the crisp, autumn night. Grant beamed as he accepted the souvenir.

"Well, young'uns," said Wilbur, closing the front door. "You just experienced a genuine Smoky Mountain shivaree! What did ya think?"

"It was fun," said Grant, playing a phantom fiddle with his new bow. "But you could've warned us that it was coming! It scared me so bad that my chill bumps got chill bumps!"

Papa put his arms around Christina's and Elizabeth's shoulders and chuckled at Grant. "But then it wouldn't have been a shivaree," he explained. "The fun is in the surprise!"

"We've had enough surprises for one day," said Christina. Since her grandparents didn't know about the clues, they didn't realize what an exciting day the kids had *before* the shivaree showed up!

The three exhausted kids climbed back up to bed and fell asleep just as their heads hit their pillows. The surprises would begin again in the morning.

13
FROST ON THE PUMPKIN!

A rooster crowed from Peg's chicken house and woke Christina early. The aroma of coffee told her that Mimi and Papa were already awake and downstairs getting ready for the day. Christina dressed quickly and suddenly realized she would have to make a trip to the dreaded outhouse!

After kissing her grandparents good morning, she put on a jacket and stepped outside. The morning was downright cold, more like winter than fall. Light frost gleamed from the meadows surrounding the cabin and the smoke rising from the mountains was thicker than what Christina noticed the day before. The white smoke and shiny frost against the blue mountains and orange-red topped trees was breathtaking. This trip to the outhouse was very different from the one last night!

In no time, Christina sauntered back to the cabin with the old hound dog trotting behind her. Suddenly, she noticed the pumpkins Elizabeth saw last night. Five pumpkins, each a different size and shape, rested in the grass next to the front porch. Pumpkins are typical outdoor decorations for autumn, she thought. But something about these looked different. And then it hit her!

A thin layer of frost topped each pumpkin! Christina remembered the clue. *A frosted pumpkin hides the way!* Could someone have known there would be frost on top of Peg and Wilbur's pumpkins? Whoever wanted Christina, Grant, and Elizabeth to find out about this mountain legend sure knew a lot about where they were visiting.

Rubbing her eyes and yawning, Elizabeth joined Christina in front of the pumpkins. "Any frosting on them this morning?" she asked jokingly.

"Not frosting," corrected Christina. "Frost! Look!"

Elizabeth squinted at the ice crystals glimmering from the top of each carrot-colored pumpkin. "Wow!" she said. "Did you find another clue?"

"Not yet," replied Christina. "Let's look around."

The girls searched and searched around the pumpkins for anything that resembled a clue, but found nothing.

"Maybe the clue wasn't talking about Peg's frosted pumpkins," said Christina, defeated.

Just as they were about to give up, Elizabeth spied what they were hunting for. "Christina, the clue isn't near the pumpkins," she declared. "It's ON the pumpkins!"

Sure enough, the frosted pumpkins held the clue. Someone had etched words in the frost on top of each of the five pumpkins.

Christina and Elizabeth high-fived each other, impressed with their detective skills. "But our guide to where?" Christina wondered aloud. "How can animals guide us to a mountain legend?"

Elizabeth's eyes widened. "Remember my grandfather's favorite Cherokee legend about the enchanted waterfall?" she asked. "I wonder if this clue means the animals could guide us to it? We could be the first humans to ever see that lake!"

The idea fascinated Christina. "You mean these clues aren't telling us about a new legend," she said, "but they could help us prove a legend we already know!"

Christina wasn't convinced they were right about where the clues were leading them. But they had two more days in the Smokies and since clues had followed them so far, she guessed they would continue. But where could they find animal guides?

14
BEAR WARNINGS AND BALD SPOTS

After an Appalachian breakfast of sweet potato pancakes drenched in Peg's homemade maple syrup, Mimi and Papa loaded the kids in the car for a trip to Cades Cove.

"Today we're visiting the Great Smoky Mountains National Park," said Papa on the drive to Cades Cove. "It's time we see these mountains up close and personal!"

"Are we going to climb up a mountain?" asked Grant.

"No, we're not climbing," replied Papa. "We're exploring the mountains! You might even end up in the middle of that Smoky Mountain smoke, Christina!"

The smile disappeared from Christina's face. She would rather be in Peg and Wilbur's outhouse than be surrounded by creepy mountain smoke.

"I hope we see a bear or a fox," said Elizabeth. "They're so cute!" Wildlife was her favorite part about visiting the mountains.

Mimi respected the wild animals of the park and she wanted to make sure the children did too. "We just might see a bear," she said. "And if we do, we will watch him from a distance! It's autumn and bears are hunting for all the food they can find to fatten up for their winter nap. We don't want to be his lunch!"

Christina leaned over to Elizabeth. "What if it's a bear that guides us to the enchanted lake?" she whispered. "I guess Mimi wouldn't be too happy about that!"

"You know, the Great Smoky Mountains National Park is one of the most visited national parks in the United States," Papa announced.

"No kidding, Papa," said Christina. "Look at all these cars! Is everyone in the country visiting the Smokies this weekend?"

Christina was right. The roads were clogged. Cars packed with tourists inched along at a snail's pace, enjoying the spectacular display of fall color in the mountains. And there was so much to see!

Autumn wildflowers painted the sides of the roads in burgundy and gold petals. Water tumbled down roadside waterfalls. Each mile marker displayed more beautiful scenery than the one before it.

The kids passed the time playing "I Spy." Christina spied a broken-down, red pickup truck next to an old barn, and white goats grazing in a meadow. Elizabeth spied a cliff of black rocks looming over the road, and a brown, wooden Great Smoky Mountains National Park sign.

Grant spied something weird. "I spy a bald old man!" he announced.

Both girls turned their heads from the window to look directly at Papa.

"Whaddaya lookin' at me for?" he cried. "I've still got a full head of hair!"

He removed his cowboy hat, stroked his short gray hair, and glanced at Grant through the rearview mirror. "And besides, who are you calling *old man*?" he asked.

"Not you, Papa!" Grant said. "The baldy I see isn't in the car. It's out there!"

Grant pointed out the window to a smooth, buttercup-yellow and green mountaintop. It was the only mountain in the entire area not covered in orange, red, and gold-leafed trees.

"So, Papa," Grant began, "why doesn't that mountain have any hair–I mean, trees?"

"Well, there are many theories," said Papa. "The Cherokee people say bald mountains formed when the Great Spirit sent a bolt of lightning down to the mountain to kill a Cherokee enemy. That left the mountain without any trees."

"Oh brother," said Grant, rolling his eyes. "Here we go with these unprovable legends again!"

Papa continued, "Scientists say that the shrubs and thickets on bald mountains are so thick, trees can't grow. Some say that grazing animals eat tree seedlings before they can grow. But the truth is, no one is completely sure why balds form."

"I guess you could say that balds are another one of the Smoky Mountains' natural mysteries," said Christina. Just like the other mysteries that are popping up on this trip, she thought.

15
BEAR PICNIC

Coneflowers and grassy meadows bordered the one-way road into Cades Cove. White-tailed deer ambled through the meadows and sometimes crossed paths with the parade of vehicles. Bicycle riders whizzed passed cars, avoiding the deer and the traffic jams.

Tucked in between the surrounding mountains, Cades Cove was once a busy farm community. The federal government established the national park in the 1930s, forcing the residents of the **vale** to leave their homes. The area became a living history lesson about early life in the Smoky Mountains and one of the most popular tourist destinations in the park.

"This house is smaller than the classroom at my school," said Christina, exploring one of the oldest homes with Grant and Elizabeth. Small and simple, the rectangular log cabin had two sets of weathered wooden shingles on its roof. One set of shingles covered the house and the second set hung over the front porch. A stone chimney stood along one wall.

"Can you imagine a family with ten to fourteen children living in this one-room house?" asked Mimi. Christina shook her head.

The kids visited a wooden barn so old and weathered it looked like it was built with toothpicks. Tattered farming equipment was still stored inside and a wagon with two broken wheels sat nearby.

"Hop on, Elizabeth!" cried Grant from the wagon seat. He snapped his arms in the air as if he was spurring horses into motion. "I'd be much obliged if you'd ride on my wagon with me!" Elizabeth and Christina jumped onto the wagon, giggling during their fantasy wagon ride.

Three quaint churches graced the loop road around Cades Cove. A cemetery full of tombstones dotted the yard alongside one little white church with a bell tower.

While they drove down Loop Road to the next historical site, Grant decided it was time for a mid-morning snack. Early that morning, Peg had packed a picnic basket full of roast beef sandwiches, ham biscuits, apples, corn salad, potato chips, and a mocha chocolate cake. Mimi insisted he save the sandwiches and the chocolate cake for lunch, so Grant passed out ham biscuits for their snack.

All three kids were devouring ham biscuits when the drive through Cades Cove came to a complete standstill. Their rental car and at least ten cars in front and behind it, stopped in the middle of the road. Passengers leaped out, many of them laughing and pointing their cameras toward some nearby woods.

"Why aren't we moving?" asked Christina. "What's everyone doing?"

"Bear jam!" announced Papa. He rolled down the car windows so the kids could get a better look.

A black bear ambled through the woods, oblivious to the chaos it had caused. Its shaggy black fur stood out against the fire-red leaves of the trees and the yellow-green shrubs.

"Papa, can we please get out of the car to watch too?" asked Christina.

"The bear seems far enough away. I guess that'd be alright," agreed Papa. "But stay close to the car!"

Scrambling out the doors, the kids left their biscuits sitting on the car seat. The animal shuffled and wandered around the woods, obviously searching for its own mid-morning snack. Suddenly, the bear lifted its snout to the air, as if it caught the scent of something floating in the breeze. It followed its nose all the way to the cars lining up to watch!

The bear lumbered down the road, sniffing the air and licking its chops. It sniffed around the windows of each car and sometimes stood on its hind legs to peer inside. As it got closer and closer, Mimi and Papa grabbed the kids by the hoods of their jackets and dragged them to a safer distance.

When the bear reached Papa's rental car, it stopped, took a long whiff, and placed its two front paws on the hood.

"Whatever that bear smells, it's in our car," said Papa.

"Our food!" cried Christina. "We left our biscuits out and the windows are open!"

The bear ambled around to the side of the car, sticking its nose into each window. In the backseat, it found what it was looking for–ham biscuits! It stuck its furry head and oversized front paws through the backseat window next to Grant's seat. With its back feet still firmly planted on the ground, the furry marauder gobbled up the half-eaten biscuits in one gulp and tipped over a thermos to slurp some sweet tea!

Probing for more food, the bear ripped apart the picnic basket with its razor-sharp claws. The lunch Peg had so lovingly packed for Mimi, Papa, and the kids rained down all over the backseat!

"I can't believe that bear is in our car!" exclaimed Mimi.

"I can't believe our lunch is being bear-napped!!" cried Christina.

"No, no! Not the chocolate cake!" pleaded Grant, watching the bear rip its tin foil wrapping to bits. "Please don't eat the cake!" Within seconds, the bear devoured the chocolate cake and every other morsel of food in the car. At the end of the feast, it yanked its head out of the backseat, glanced around at the stunned crowd, and slowly sauntered back into the woods.

Mimi, Papa, and the kids hurried to the car to survey the damage. Bear claw marks ripped through the paint on one door. But the real disaster was inside. Splintered sections of the picnic basket were tossed everywhere. Ripped tin foil and cellophane wrapping littered the seats and floors. The flattened thermos dripped sticky rivers of sweet tea down the back of Papa's seat. Not a single morsel remained. The bear had licked them all up!

"GROSS!" exclaimed Christina. "There's bear drool on my backpack!"

"I guess bears don't have the best table manners," said Elizabeth, giggling.

"Well, we shared our lunch with a bear after all," said Mimi, exasperated.

After cleaning up the best they could, Papa had an idea. "Let's drive to the picnic area near the Abrams Falls hiking trails," he said. "You kids can explore the trails and streams and Mimi and I can find a substitute lunch!"

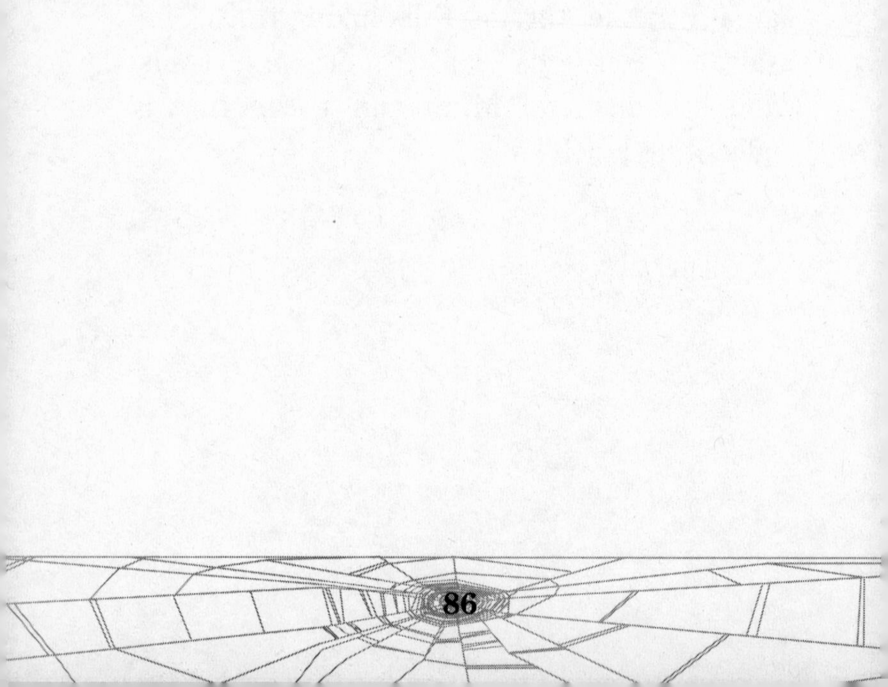

16
SKUNK RODEO!

Elizabeth spied a familiar face at the picnic area near the Abrams Falls trailhead. "Grandpa!" she cried, hurdling out of the car. She threw her arms around Carter Morgan's neck and he twirled her around in the air. "What are you doing here?"

"I wanted to spend the day with y'all," Carter replied. "I got someone to step in for the school tours. So, I called Papa last night and told him I'd surprise you young'uns here this morning!"

"It's perfect timing, Carter," said Papa. "A black bear just made mincemeat of our car and robbed us of our lunch! We'll need your help to get our sightseeing back on track."

The adults walked over to the car to show Carter evidence of the bear's picnic and made arrangements to get more food.

Christina, Grant, and Elizabeth inspected the base of the trails leading to Abrams Falls. They climbed rocks, trotted across bridges, jumped over small streams, and played hide and seek in the woods.

"Ready or not, here I come!" shouted Elizabeth.

Grant crouched down behind a jagged boulder, certain he was well hidden.

Within seconds, someone shouted, "I found you!"

"Rats!" said Grant. A man wearing a neatly trimmed black beard, army-green pants and gray shirt had discovered his hiding place. A round, wide-brimmed gray hat perched on top of his head. The gold badge pinned to his shirt read National Park Ranger.

"Great hiding spot," said the ranger. "I've used that one myself!"

"Are you playing hide and seek with us?" asked Grant, confused.

The ranger shook his head and replied, "No! My name is Cody Daniels and I'm a wildlife specialist here at Cades Cove. Your grandparents over there said y'all might want to help me with a skunk rodeo!"

A smile flashed across Grant's face. "A skunk rodeo?" he asked. Images of skunks wearing cowboy hats and riding bucking broncos filled his head. "Do you mean a rodeo with bull riding and calf roping?"

Ranger Daniels laughed at Grant's question. "No! Not that kind of rodeo!" he said. "It's more like a round-up...a round-up of skunks."

Christina and Elizabeth saw Grant talking with the man in uniform, mistaking him for a police office. "Wonder what he did this time," said Christina, worried that her brother might be in trouble.

"Officer, I can explain about my brother," Christina said to the ranger. "He's young and we weren't watching him and..."

"Wait a minute!" interrupted Grant, glaring at his sister. "I didn't do anything!

Ranger Daniels wants us to help him round up skunks!"

"Why do we have to round up skunks?" asked Elizabeth.

"Well," said Ranger Daniels, "we've had a population explosion of skunks around Abrams Falls recently. There have been too many reports of tourists being sprayed by a surprised skunk. So, we need to relocate some of them to a less populated area about fifteen miles from here. Hopefully, that will cut down on the chances for tourist-skunk meetings!"

"Sounds like a smelly job to me!" said Grant. "How can we round them up without getting shot with stink ourselves?"

"Come on," said the ranger, waving his arm for the kids to follow. "I'll explain on our way to the picnic area."

Just as Ranger Daniels predicted, a group of skunks scavenged around the tables and trashcans of the picnic area searching for food. He handed each child a set of heavy work gloves to wear.

The skunk rodeo was underway!

Ranger Daniels darted from one end of the picnic area to the other with a blowgun, puffing tranquilizer darts into unsuspecting skunks. The skunks immediately zonked out and fell to the ground. Grant, Christina, and Elizabeth swooped in to collect the snoozing critters and placed them carefully into holding cages. "Can you believe this?" Grant cried in delight. "They're dropping like flies!"

"Don't forget!" the ranger called. "Skunks can't spray unless their tail is up in the air! So fold their tails down over their rear ends before you pick them up. Otherwise, they could accidentally spray in their sleep!"

The kids worked quickly, folding fluffy tails over smelly shooters and placing knocked-out skunks into cages. When all the cages were full, the kids helped Ranger Daniels carry the sleeping skunks to a truck ready to move them to their new home.

Christina shoved the last cage into the truck when Grant noticed two or three skunks stirring from their sleep.

"Oh no!" cried Grant. "They're waking up! We're going to get squirted!"

The tranquilizers were wearing off and soon the truck would be full of confused, drugged, angry skunks ready to attack with their stinky sprayers!

"Get back, kids!" warned Ranger Daniels.

The kids hid behind a nearby tree. Ranger Daniels ran to close the tailgate of the truck. Just before the tailgate slammed shut, one woozy, scared skunk pointed its fanny at the ranger and fired its putrid mist all over him!

"PEEEYOOOOWEEEEE!" Grant cried. "That is nasty, nasty, nasty!"

The ranger smiled sheepishly and wiped his face with a handkerchief. "I guess I'll have to ride with the windows down!" he said as he climbed behind the steering wheel. "Thanks for being my skunk rodeo **allies**! I couldn't have done it without you!"

He pulled the truck out onto the road, racing to drop his furry, black-and-white cargo at their new home.

"He'll need other skunk cowboys to help wrangle those critters out of his truck," said Christina. "But who will to want to help a reeking ranger?"

17

OLD-TIMEY SPACESHIP?

While the skunk rodeo occurred under Carter's watchful eye, Mimi and Papa picked up a replacement lunch and returned to set up a picnic. Even though the substitute sandwiches weren't as yummy as Peg's "bear-wiches," the kids gobbled them up anyway. Rounding up skunks made them hungry!

After a quick tour of the grist mill and other historic Cades Cove buildings, the group headed north to Laurel Falls. The popular waterfall's hiking trail was an easy climb and would be fun for the whole group.

At the trailhead, Christina, Elizabeth, and Grant snuck off on their own to talk about the clue the girls found that morning.

"How are we going to find animals to guide us to this legend?" wondered Christina. "Well, we've had major run-ins with animals so far today," said Elizabeth. "Maybe one of them was the 'animal' the pumpkin clue talked about."

"Well, I don't remember that bear asking us to follow him when he ransacked our car!" said Grant. "And I sure wasn't going anywhere with those stinky skunks."

A smile crossed Christina's face. "The more I think about it, the more I am sure these clues will lead us to that enchanted lake your grandfather told us about," she said. "But I don't think we'll find it around here."

"Why not?" asked Elizabeth.

"I'll have to tell you later," said Christina, returning her grandfather's wave. "It's time to hit the trails!"

"The biodiversity of the Smokies is all around us," said Carter, as they hiked up the path to Laurel Falls. "Hundreds of thousands of species of trees, plants, shrubs, and fungi live in these mountains!"

Lush laurel bushes, their pink and white blooms gone since summer, decorated the hills and woods around the path. A little farther up the path, rhododendron bushes, vines, and wildflowers wove in and out of the pine and oak trees. Christina was pleased not to find any of the eerie mountain smoke along their hiking trail. Smoke could turn a lovely hike into something a little more sinister.

As they moved up the trail, Grant detoured from the path to explore a thicket of trees. After a few minutes, Christina noticed that her brother had not returned to their group. Knowing Mimi and Papa would not approve of him exploring on his own, she backtracked to find him before her grandparents could notice.

"Grant!" she called. "Grant, where are you?"

From deep in the woods, she heard her brother's reply. "I'm over here, Christina!" he yelled back. "I found a cool doohickey!!!"

Christina followed the sound of Grant's voice. He stood in the middle of a laurel thicket next to a contraption unlike any she had ever seen. "It's gotta be an old-timey rocket ship or something!" he said, inspecting the "rocket" from top to bottom.

At the center of the contraption, a squatty metal pot with a narrow neck sat on a metal rack. Underneath the rack was a pile of ash, a clue that a fire once burned there. From the top of the squatty pot, hoses snaked out in two directions. One hose looped over to an open galvanized metal bucket resting on the ground. The other hose spiraled down into the top of a tall metal can sitting on a square box. One additional hose ran from the bottom of the metal can into a clay jug.

"That thing isn't going to blast into space, Grant," said Christina.

"Well then, smarty pants," Grant said, "if it's not a rocket, what is it?"

Before Christina could reply, Papa arrived in the woods with Mimi, Carter, and Elizabeth trailing behind. He looked irritated. "Grant and Christina!" he bellowed. "You know better than to...well, lookey there!"

When he saw the rustic machine, Papa forgot all about his exasperation with his grandchildren. "You two have made quite a discovery!" he announced. "That's a moonshine still!"

"Ha! I was right!" Grant exclaimed, pumping his bony arm in the air. "This thing is a rocket that goes to the moon!"

Papa patted his grandson on the shoulder. "Sorry, youngster," he said. "It doesn't travel to the moon. But it does make what mountain folks call moonshine–which is hard grain alcohol."

"I don't get it," said Elizabeth, investigating the hoses and buckets. "Why did people make alcohol all the way up here in the mountains? Why didn't they make it in their house?"

Carter tried to give a simple explanation. "For lots of reasons, one of them being health reasons. Folks aren't supposed to make their own alcohol to drink," he explained. "So, moonshiners would find a hiding place in the mountains and build these homemade stills. They made alcohol at night so no one would catch them."

"Ohhhh," said Grant. "They made it while the moon shined!" He still didn't understand what the big deal was about making moonshine, but adults were weird about stuff like that sometimes.

The group resumed their hike up to Laurel Falls. They crossed babbling mountain streams and passed pine trees twisted like corkscrews from the heavy winds that blow at the mountain's higher elevations. The roar of tumbling water met their ears as the hikers approached a misty waterfall. Christina, Grant, and Elizabeth stepped through a tunnel of trees out onto a rock ledge. The site of the falls was breathtaking!

No one spoke for a few minutes, mesmerized by the glistening threads of water cascading down. At the top of the falls, water shot over the rocks in a fury and stair-stepped down moss-covered boulders to the pool below.

Christina could have stared at Laurel Falls for hours. How could an enchanted lake be any more beautiful than this?

18
BEE STING

"But I don't wanna go to a quilting bee!" cried Grant, when they returned to the car. "What kind of fun can a kid have watching people sew blankets?"

It had been an exciting day herding skunks, trekking to waterfalls, and even cleaning up after a bear disaster. Mimi's plans for the evening sounded a little dull to Grant.

"Grant, quilting bees are my favorite Smoky Mountain tradition," Mimi said, making notes in her red leather journal.

"Ok, Mimi," said Grant. "If it's important to you, I'll go. But I still don't think it sounds fun."

Carter and Elizabeth drove back to Penland School for the night, with plans to meet Mimi, Papa, and the kids the next morning for more adventures around the park. Mimi and Papa planned to meet Peg at her monthly quilting bee held in a local church hall.

As Mimi, Papa, and Christina walked up the steps of the church, Grant noticed a most unusual sight.

"Mimi!" he called. "There's someone in a space suit walking around behind the church!" He followed the suit to see where it was going.

"Grant, you'll say just about anything to avoid this quilting bee, won't you?" asked Christina. She assured her grandparents she would bring Grant inside, and skipped down the church stairs to collect her brother.

Behind the church, the "spaceman" waddled over to a fat oak tree. Several large wooden boxes sat on tables beneath its branches. Christina caught up with Grant and saw what he meant about the space suit! The person under the tree was dressed in a white coverall with white gloves and black boots. A white square-shaped box covered the person's head like a hood. Black netting ran across the front.

The "spaceman" noticed Christina and Grant watching and marched over to the kids. "You kids shouldn't be here," a woman's voice said sternly. "It could be dangerous."

The lady inside the suit took off the square hood that covered her face and head. Her strawberry blond curls exploded around her face when released from her hood. She smiled at the kids with a bucktooth grin and a wink.

"We were just wondering what you were doing," said Grant sheepishly. "Why are you dressed like that?"

"Why, I have to dress in these threads to take care of what's inside those boxes," she replied. "My name is Ida. What's you'uns?"

Grant and Christina introduced themselves and explained that they had come with their grandparents for the quilting bee.

"How 'bout I show you what's in those boxes 'fore you go to that quilting bee?" offered Ida. "But you'll have to put these duds on too. C'mon!"

Grant was thrilled! Dressing in a space suit to investigate some boxes beat a boring old quilting bee any day! The kids donned bulky white coveralls over their jeans and sweatshirts, pulled on white gloves, and wiggled the boxy hood down over their faces. They looked like three astronauts on a moonwalk!

Waddling toward the wooden boxes under the tree, Grant bumped into Christina three times. "Sorry!" he said, giggling. "I can't see a thing in this hood!"

As they neared the tree, the kids heard a loud humming sound from inside the boxes.

"All right," Ida instructed, "stand next to me but don't touch anything. Just watch." In one hand, she held a small metal can with smoke curling out of a narrow hole. She unlatched the lock on one box and opened the lid. The humming grew louder.

Christina's mouth dropped open behind her black netting. Inside the box, thousands of bees crawled around a honeycomb. A few bees escaped into the air and dive-bombed Grant's head. He flinched and swatted in the air, forgetting that the suit and his netted hood protected him from being stung.

"I am an apiarist," said Ida. "That's a beekeeper! I take care of beehives and collect the honey the bees make in their honeycombs. Sometimes farmers use my bees to pollinate their plants and crops."

Ida sprayed smoke around the hives to keep the bees from getting too active and swarming around Grant and Christina.

"It's fun to watch bees up close and not worry about being stung," said Christina. Black bees crept all over her white suit.

The kids watched Ida as she worked with the bees and collected the honey from the honeycomb. When her work was done, she latched the last box. "OK, kiddos," she said. "Let's get changed."

Suddenly, Grant let out a yelp and began to flail his arms in the air.

"It's OK, Grant," said Christina, "Remember, the bees can't sting you while you're wearing the protective suit!"

"But there's a bee INSIDE my suit!" he cried.

A bee had worked its way through a hole in Grant's hood and was now buzzing around his face. Ida calmly removed Grant's hood to swat the bee away, but it was too late.

"YEEE OWWWW!" he cried. The bee stung him right on the tip of his nose. Grant ran straight for the church, one hand over his nose and the other hand swatting at the air to ensure other bees weren't after him.

"I look like Rudolph the Red-Nosed Reindeer," said Grant, angrily yanking off his coveralls. A huge blister rose on his watermelon-red nose.

Grant and Christina thanked Ida for their bee encounter and headed into the church to find their grandparents and the quilting bee.

Mimi took one look at him and rushed to his side. "Grant!" she said. "What happened to your nose?"

Christina told Mimi about Ida and the bees.

"Mimi," whined Grant. "My nose hurts!"

"Don't worry," assured Mimi. "I'll bet Peg knows just what to do."

Papa found Peg and told her what happened to Grant. Peg nodded and smiled at Papa, then disappeared from the room for a few minutes. When she returned, she held a small cloth pouch stuffed with a wet, gooey, purple substance inside.

"Here you go, hon," said Peg. "Stick this on your nose. It's a special recipe of flowers and roots and it'll take that sting away in no time!"

Grant looked at his grandmother with concern. This wasn't like any medicine Mimi had ever given him. Mimi smiled, took the gooey cloth from Peg, and handed it to Grant. "Mountain remedies work on mountain ailments, Grant," said Mimi. "Now put this on your nose."

Grant stuck the squishy pouch on the tip of his nose. "Eww!" he complained. "This smells worse than the skunks at the rodeo!"

Christina giggled at her brother's predicament. "Grant, you really know how to put the BEE into quilting bee!" she joked.

Grant scowled at his sister from behind the smelly bag of bee-sting fixer. But within five minutes, the pain went away and his nose returned to its normal size.

Mimi smiled and thanked Peg for her help. "Aww, my pleasure," said Peg. "Up here in the mountains, we've always got a cure for what ails ya!"

19

CALICO CLUE

Grant decided that looking at colorful, handmade patterned quilts was better than holding stinky medicine on his nose. He was happy to be at Mimi's quilting bee after all.

The quilting bee was in full swing in the cozy church hall. Fifteen women sat in chairs, furiously sewing stitches into squares of fabric. As soon as one quilter stitched several squares together, she handed her section to another quilter to connect to their section. This process continued until an entire patchwork of squares linked to form the soft, comforting outside of a blanket.

Christina noticed that quilting wasn't the only activity happening in the church hall.

The ladies were also laughing and singing, talking and listening, and teaching and learning. Mimi and Papa plopped right in the middle of the group, enjoying every minute.

When Christina stood next to her grandmother, Mimi grabbed her hand and squeezed hard. "This is what I love about the mountain way of life," she said. "Quilting bees have been an important part of women's lives for centuries! They gathered to make quilts to keep their families warm during harsh mountain winters. But the bee became a time of giving and sharing. Quilters shared stories, passed along information, taught the young ones to sew, shared a meal, and socialized. The quilts they made symbolize that friendship and togetherness."

Christina smiled at Mimi and wrapped her in a quick hug. She saw Grant standing at the back of the church hall jumping and waving his hands in the air. She wandered back to see why Grant was going crazy.

"What's wrong with you?" asked Christina. "Did a bee sting your backside this time?"

"Very funny," answered Grant. He pointed at a quilt hanging from a rack on the wall. "You're gonna want to see this!"

Christina peered at the stunning counterpane quilt made with multicolored squares of calico fabric. "It's pretty," said Christina, not sure what the big deal was about.

"Look at the squares!" urged Grant.

Christina inspected the fabric sewn into the quilt. Every other calico square had an animal on it, like bears, birds, lizards, squirrels, and deer. Triangle patterns connected the animal patterns. Each triangle pointed in the same direction, as if they were directional arrows.

Christina traced her finger from animal-square to animal-square, following the direction of the arrows. She remembered the message on the pumpkins. The animals will guide you. Maybe they weren't looking for real animals; they were looking for quilted animals! Her finger stopped on the only square with a different pattern–a lake! She felt something bulky behind the lake design. Inspecting closely, Christina noticed that the square was not sewn on all four sides.

It was a pocket! But what was inside? Gently, she pulled the top of the square away from the quilt to reveal a piece of folded calico tucked inside. Unfolding the fabric, Christina read the words that were stitched on its surface.

"Elizabeth was right!" said Christina. "These clues are leading us to the enchanted waterfall and lake. They really exist! The legend must be true!"

"Now all we need to do is find a dome and look under it," said Grant. "Are there any domes around here?"

"Just the one that formed on your nose when that bee stung you!" teased Christina.

Grant would have given his sister a friendly punch in the arm if Papa hadn't interrupted to say it was time to leave. It would be another fun-filled night at Peg and Wilbur's house.

20

AIN'T IT HAINTED?

Mimi and Papa walked hand in hand along the split-rail fence crossing Peg and Wilbur's meadow. They watched the sunset dip silently below the mountains when Grant ran out to the meadow yelling and waving.

"Mimi! Papa! Mimi! Papa!" he shouted.

"What in the name of tar and molasses is going on with you, young man?" Papa asked, alarmed.

Grant gasped to catch his breath. "Wilbur just told me...about a hiking trail... we've got to visit!" he sputtered. "Promise me...we can go tomorrow! I just have to...hike this trail! Please!"

"Slow down, Grant!" urged Mimi. "Slow down and tell us what in the world you're talking about."

Grant took a deep breath and began again. "Wilbur told me about a hiking trail that's not too far away from here," he said. "I just have to hike on this trail. I just have to!"

"What's so great about this trail?" asked Papa.

"Because it's called BOOGERMAN'S Trail!" exclaimed Grant, hooting with laughter. "BOOGERMAN'S! Can you believe that's a guy's name?"

"Oh Grant!" said Mimi, bending down to retie her red, high-top tennis shoes. "We are not going to any Boogerman Trail tomorrow."

Grant giggled when he heard his grandmother say "Boogerman."

"Nope," said Papa. "We've got other plans for tomorrow. Boogerman's will have to wait for another time."

"Do you think the guy who found that trail picked his nose all the time?" asked

Grant. He laughed as he scampered back to the house to find his sister. Wait until I tell Christina about that trail, he thought. It'll gross her out!

After another dinner feast prepared by Peg, Wilbur offered to take their houseguests out for a tractor ride and night hike up into the hills at the base of the nearby mountain.

Mimi, Papa, and Grant immediately said yes. Christina hesitated. Those mountains scared her at night. What if that creepy smoke was there again? She went, but she wasn't happy about it.

Armed with flashlights and bundled in jackets and quilts, they hopped onto the wagon hitched to Wilbur's tractor. The tractor motor sputtered to life and the wagon jolted and jutted across the meadow. The full moon hung so low over the mountains, it looked like a rock Grant could grab and throw into a stream.

Christina snuggled close to Papa and felt a little safer out in the dark. Her eyes darted all around the mountains, searching for spooky smoke that could surround them at any minute. The wagon lurched to a stop at the base of the mountain.

"We're not going far," promised Wilbur, leading the night hike. "Just high enough to see how purdy the moon shines on our little holler."

With only the moonlight and flashlights to guide them, the group hiked to a clearing at the top of a hill. The sounds of snapping sticks and twigs under their feet echoed into the mountains. Branches of rhododendron bushes reached out like ghostly fingers to grab them as they walked by. Christina could see an owl's yellow eyes glaring from a low tree branch. The owl let out a long, low *hoo hoo* into the night air.

"The overlook is right through them trees," called Wilbur, his finger pointing in the moonlight. Christina saw a spooky orange glow rising up through the trees. Shivers climbed up her spine and she grabbed Papa's hand as they hiked right toward it. Suddenly, she felt something crawling up her back. Christina gasped and spun around in fear.

"Gotcha!" teased Grant, wiggling five fingers in the air.

"NOT funny, Grant," said Christina. She grabbed Papa's hand again as they approached the trees.

Christina was overjoyed when they entered the clearing and saw the warm glow of a roaring campfire. The fiddle player from last night's shivaree was standing there, his fiddle propped on a rock. He tossed in two logs, causing the fire to crackle and snap. Embers and sparks danced in the night air.

From her bag, Peg pulled out marshmallows, chocolate bars, and graham crackers.

"Yum! S'mores!" said Grant, licking his lips.

Christina and Grant flopped onto the dirt next to the fire and roasted marshmallows as the fiddler lifted his instrument. Tonight his bow swayed slowly across the strings, sending sweet music into the mountains.

Christina finally relaxed and enjoyed being outside. The fire, the music, and the s'mores made the mountain fun instead of creepy!

Wilbur sat down next to the kids. "Y'all know there's haints up in these hills," he said.

"Haints?" repeated Christina, her eyes wide and staring at Wilbur.

"Wilbur Walker," scolded Peg. "Don't you go off scarin' these young'uns."

Grant licked gooey marshmallow off his fingers. "I'm not scared," said Grant. "What's a haint?"

"A ghost!" said Wilbur, smiling a sinister smile.

"Oh," said Grant. He wasn't feeling so brave anymore.

Wilbur continued, "During the Civil War, five families lived in this holler. Thar was one set of newlyweds. The husband enlisted in the Confederate Army the day after he married his bride. The bride was heartbroken when her husband left and she cried for two months straight.

"Finally, she decided she'd find her husband and take care of him on the battlefield," Wilbur added. "She set off walking toward Virginia in search of his regiment. But they say she got lost in these mountain woods. No one ever heard from her again. Her haint still roams these hills, searching for her husband. Sometimes you can hear her voice calling for him in the wind and in the rustling leaves."

"I ain't never seen a haint!" said Grant, gathering up leftover marshmallows and roasting sticks. "And I don't want to see one tonight!"

Christina felt cold, even next to the warm fire. She thought about the bride walking alone in the mountains at night and her shoulders began to quiver. She was ready to go back to the cabin and snuggle up under a warm, safe quilt.

Wilbur poured a bucket of cold water on the fire and the hikers set off down the trail to the waiting wagon. The wind shook the leaves of the trees and a faint whine like that of a crying woman floated into the mountains.

21
VIEW FROM THE TOP OF THE WORLD

The next morning before the sun was up, Mimi, Papa, Christina, and Grant met Carter and Elizabeth in a parking lot at a trailhead located in the center of Great Smoky Mountains National Park.

"It's the middle of the night!" whined Grant, yawning and stretching.

"It's almost sunrise, Grant," said Mimi. "Trust me! You won't want to sleep through this!"

The kids followed the adults up the steep hiking trail. Grant's heart pounded from the strenuous climb. He was wide awake now! The yellow glow of the rising sun was beginning to appear over the mountaintops.

"Let's hurry," said Papa, quickening his step. "We don't want to miss it!"

The group arrived at a concrete ramp and followed it as it circled above the treetops. At the top of the ramp was an observation tower. The kids huddled along the edge of the tower and gazed out over the shadowy mountains.

"There it is!" exclaimed Papa, pointing toward the mountains.

They watched the sun inch up over the horizon and bathe the mountains in morning light. With every minute, Christina could see farther and farther across the mountain range standing tall against the bright blue sky.

Tints of orange, gold, red, green, and blue spread patterns across the mountain range. The view looked like a counterpane quilt of colors made by Mother Nature herself.

"Wow!" said Grant. "It feels like we're on top of the world!" He ran around the observation tower, which displayed a 360-degree view of the Great Smoky Mountains.

"On a clear day, you can see seven states from this observation tower," said

Carter, his arm around Elizabeth's shoulder. "And this morning is the clearest I've seen in a long while!"

The kids listed the states they thought they could see in the distance. "North Carolina, Tennessee, Virginia, South Carolina,..." they began.

"I feel like I can see all the way to Alaska from here!" joked Elizabeth.

The sight of the sun rising over the mountains made Grant burst into song, "On top of ol' Smoky! All covered with cheese! I lost my poor meatball! When somebody sneezed!"

Christina and Mimi covered their ears. "Please don't ruin this beautiful morning with your singing, Grant!" complained Christina.

"Papa, where are we anyway?" asked Grant when he finished his song. They began their travels so early that morning, he and Christina were too sleepy to care about their destination.

"We're at Clingman's Dome," said Papa. "It's the highest peak in the Smoky Mountains."

Christina smacked Grant on the arm and whispered, "The clue from the quilt said, 'The lake you seek is under the dome.' And Carter's legend said the enchanted waterfall could be found beneath the trees at the Smoky Mountains' highest peak."

"The lake has to be close by!" Grant whispered back.

"Grab Elizabeth," Christina instructed Grant. "We've gotta tell her about the clue we found last night and then find that lake!"

22
SO CLOSE!

The adults chatted at the observation tower while the kids scampered down the ramp to the trail below.

"Stay close by," warned Papa. His grandchildren had a habit of wandering off and he didn't want any of that nonsense today.

Christina and Grant told Elizabeth about the clue they found at the quilting bee and their theory that the enchanted lake was located near Clingman's Dome.

"You must be right!" exclaimed Elizabeth. "We need to listen for falling water or look for animal tracks. Those clues could lead us right to the lake."

The kids fanned out from the hiking path into the trees. They searched for anything that might point the way to a lake surrounded by animals.

Christina watched as a hawk circled low above the hemlock trees. It sees something, she thought. She walked in its direction.

"I just saw three raccoons run into those hemlock trees over there!" called Elizabeth, pointing in the same direction as the hawk.

"I found animal footprints!" called Grant. "I don't know what kind of animals they are, but there are tons of them!"

Christina and Elizabeth raced over to Grant. Hundreds of animal tracks marked the ground, and all were going in the same direction–into the hemlock trees at the base of Clingman's Dome!

As the kids followed the tracks, a loud snorting and shuffling sound startled them. Christina grabbed Grant and Elizabeth and ducked behind a bush. "That sure sounds like a bear to me," said Christina.

She was right! A small black bear climbed down from its perch in a treetop and began lumbering through the woods.

"He must be looking for some breakfast," whispered Elizabeth.

As the bear stopped to crunch on some acorns, Christina noticed a bloody, red stripe across the top of its nose.

"Look," said Christina. "He's got a bad cut on his snout."

"That looks like it hurts," said Grant. "Too bad I don't have one of Peg's stinky mountain medicine pouches for him!"

After two or three handfuls of acorns, the bear dropped the rest of his snack and shuffled off into the trees.

"The coast is clear," said Elizabeth. "Let's go!"

The kids resumed the trail through the thick brush, following the animal tracks with newly added bear prints. In front of a rhododendron bush at the base of a hemlock tree, the animal tracks abruptly stopped. So did the kids.

"Where did they go?" Christina asked, frantically looking around.

"How could they just...just...disappear?" asked Elizabeth.

Grant held his hand in the air, motioning the girls. "Listen!" he said.

In the cool, early morning air, Christina, Elizabeth, and Grant heard the sound of flowing water. It was the same sound they heard at Laurel Falls, as the water from the falls dumped into the pool below.

"It's gotta be the lake!" exclaimed Elizabeth. "It's real! It's real! These animals must be there!"

Out of the corner of her eye, Christina noticed a white, smoky mist rising above the nearby hemlock trees. For once, she was happy to see the mountain smoke. It must be rising off the lake, she thought!

"The smoke is rising off the lake!" shouted Christina. "All we have to do is follow it!"

Just as the three kids started tearing through the trees toward the sounds and the smoke, a booming voice called out.

"Are you kids looking for something?" called Carter. He had a gleam in his eyes and a broad smile across his face.

Mimi and Papa marched up right behind him. They were not pleased that the children had wandered so far off the path.

"Uhhh, ummmm," sputtered Grant. "We were just exploring."

"I told you kids to stay close to that path," scolded Papa. "This place is filled with wild animals and dangerous drop-offs. You could get hurt out here."

Not if we found a magical lake that could heal wounds, thought Christina. She looked over her shoulder to see if the hawk still circled in the sky. It was gone. The smoke disappeared and the sound of the water had stopped too. They had been so close to finding that enchanted waterfall! Now it seemed like it had disappeared right in front of them.

As Papa, Mimi, and Carter led them back to the hiking trail, Grant asked his grandmother a question. "Mimi, do you think the legend about the lake that heals wounded animals is true?" he asked. "I mean, is that lake real?"

"What made you think of that again?" asked Mimi, unaware of her grandchildren's trail of clues.

"Well, Carter said it could be found at the base of the Smokies' highest peak," said Grant. "If Clingman's Dome is the Smokies' highest peak, then that lake should be around here."

"Grant," said Mimi, patting the top of her grandson's head, "I think if an enchanted lake existed, these magical mountains would be the perfect place for it!"

Christina looked at Carter, who still had a goofy grin on his face. She wasn't positive but he looked like he knew exactly what they had been searching for at the base of Clingman's Dome.

"Look!" Papa called. "There's a bear walking near those trees!" The group stopped to watch a small black bear amble through the woods looking for acorns and berries.

“Is that the bear we saw earlier?” Grant asked the girls in a whisper so the grownups couldn’t hear.

“I don’t know,” said Elizabeth. “But this one’s fur is all wet. He must have just taken a swim!”

“It is the same bear!” said Christina. “Look at his nose!”

A thin white scar laid across the top of the bear’s snout where a cut had healed.

The kids looked at one another in amazement. They hadn’t found the enchanted lake that could heal wounds, but it sure seemed that the bear had! Christina nodded at the bear, and smiled.

23
MOUNTAIN JAMBOREE!

"Who's ready for a mountain jamboree?" asked Papa, happily rocking back and forth in his rocking chair at LeConte Lodge. The group's arrival to Mount LeConte that evening was a challenge since the only way to get to the lodge is to hike there on foot!

Earlier in the day, Christina, Grant, Elizabeth, and Carter hiked to the top of Mount LeConte by way of the steep but scenic trail. Mimi and Papa caught a ride with the llamas that haul food and supplies up to the lodge several times a week. Both treks to the lodge were long but the payoff was worth it! Perched atop one of the Smokies' highest peaks, they watched the glowing sun dip below the hazy blue mountains.

"We've seen the sunrise AND the sunset over these mountains today!" said Grant, licking the barbeque sauce off his fingers. He had just finished his first helping of the grand feast served outside on Myrtle Point and was about go get seconds!

Three fiddlers gathered nearby, and soon the fiddles came alive with foot-stompin' mountain music. Christina and Elizabeth weren't too shy to join the party this time! They led their grandparents to the grass which served as a dance floor. Papa and Carter spun their granddaughters around in a circle. Someone handed Mimi a pair of spoons and she bounced them off her knee in time to the beat. It was a bona fide mountain hootenanny with home cooking, home-grown vittles, and homespun music!

Christina stopped dancing for a moment and looked out over the Smoky Mountains. They may not have found an enchanted lake today, but she realized every cove, waterfall, forest, animal, and plant in these mountains was magical. She knew now why Mimi loved mountain life and the traditions of the people who lived there.

Wisps of smoke fluttered into the autumn air, floating over the fiery oranges and golds of the mighty and magical mountains. Christina smiled at the sight of the smoke. What other legends hid behind its mysterious mist???

Well, that was fun!

Wow, glad we solved that mystery!

Where shall we go next?

EVERYWHERE!

The End

Now...go to

www.carolemarshmysteries.com

and...

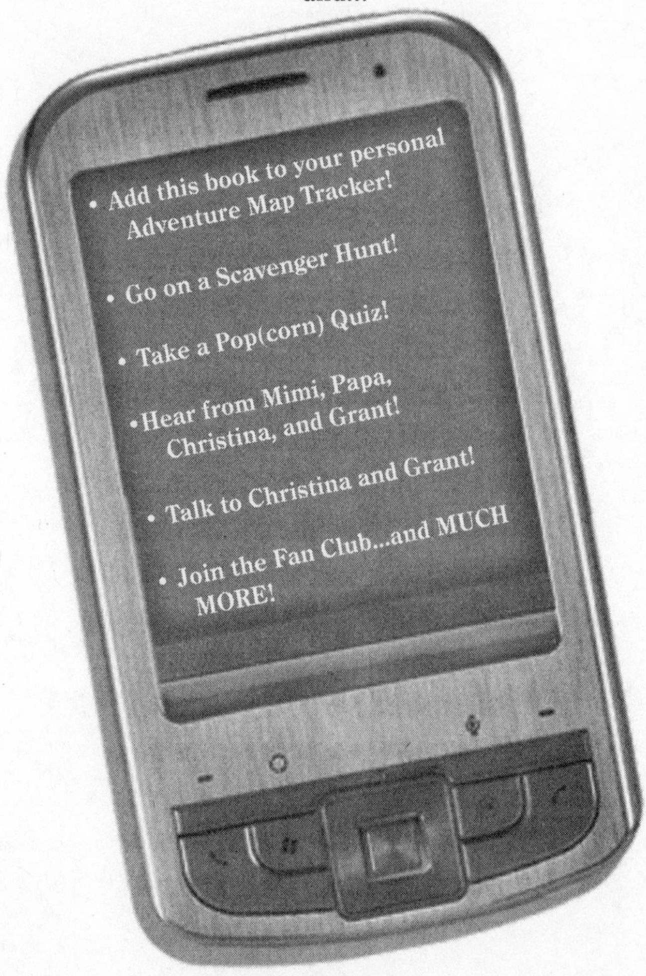

GLOSSARY

biodiversity: a variety of plant and animal species in an environment

coverall: a loose-fitting, one-piece work garment

fluent: able to speak smoothly or easily

galvanized: coated with a rust-resistant zinc

heritage: something passed down from a previous generation; a tradition

intricate: complex, detailed

putrid: in a state of decay or rot; having a rotten odor

rustic: charmingly simple or unsophisticated

SAT GLOSSARY

ally: a person or thing connected with another, usually in some relation of helpfulness

probe: to search through and through

tranquil: calm

vale: level or low land between hills

vista: a view, especially one seen through a long, narrow passage, as between rows of trees or houses

Enjoy this exciting excerpt from:

THE MYSTERY ON THE Great Lakes

What I Did on My Vacation
by Grant

We went to the Great Lakes. It was great! If you don't know where they are, well, they are across the top of the United States, on the border between us and Canada. If you don't know how to remember the Great Lakes, just think: HOMES–Huron, Ontario, Michigan, Erie, and Superior. The Great Lakes are so great that you really can't see from one side to another. They really seem more like oceans, especially on stormy days.

We went from one lake to the other on a big adventure with my sister, Christina, and my grandparents, Mimi and Papa. I learned a lot about shipwrecks, sand dunes, and scary stuff like haunted lighthouses. The Great Lakes have a LOT of lighthouses. I'm not sure how much good they do, because the Great Lakes also have a lot of shipwrecks. A LOT of shipwrecks!

1
WHEN BUFFALOES FLY

Christina wiped her mouth with a bright yellow napkin. The spicy hot sauce from the Buffalo wings stung her lips and tickled her tongue. Her blue eyes watered until tears streaked her cheeks.

Grant grinned, his mouth coated with greasy orange sauce. "These are great! But I didn't know buffaloes had wings." Buffalo sauce covered his hands and trickled down his arms to his elbows.

"Eww, Grant," Christina said. She handed him a napkin.

Mimi laughed. "Glad you like them," she said, "but buffaloes don't have wings. Buffalo wings are chicken. They're named

Buffalo wings because they were created right here, in Buffalo, New York!"

Even eating the messy Buffalo wings, Mimi kept her white ruffled blouse and red suit jacket spotless. She somehow didn't seem bothered by the super-spicy hot sauce either.

Papa took several long gulps of lemonade. He'd ordered the hottest hot wings, and from the look on his face, they were fiery hot! Of course, Mimi always said he had a mouth made of stainless steel. He could eat–and enjoy–even hot jalapeño peppers.

"Papa, when are we going to see the Rock and Roll Hall of Fame?" Christina asked.

"We'll be there in no time," Papa replied, his voice hoarse from the hot sauce. "We're just about ready to kick off our tour of the Great Lakes!"

Grant and Christina often traveled with their mystery-writing grandmother, Mimi, as she did research for her books. Her latest book was to be set on the Great Lakes. Their grandfather, Papa, flew the family wherever they needed to go in his red-and-white airplane, the *Mystery Girl*. Mimi affectionately referred to him as the "cowboy pilot" in his Stetson hat, jeans, and leather boots.

Papa took one last gulp from his tall drink. "Once we finish lunch," he explained, "we're off to board the *Mystery Girl*. She'll take us over to Cleveland and Lake Erie."

"*Eeeeerie*?? That's a creepy name for a lake. Where were we earlier today?" Grant asked.

"Lake Ontario," Christina said. Don't you remember, Papa said our route would be Lake Ontario, then southwest to Lake Erie, then north to Lake Huron, then more north to Lake Superior, then south to Lake Michigan, or vice versa, I forget."

Grant groaned. "Well, I'm lost already. I can see I won't be able to write my 'What I Did on My Vacation' report next year in school without a big, giant map!"

"Niagara Falls sure was pretty this morning," Papa said. He wiped a bead of sweat from his brow, still feeling the effects of the hot sauce. He grabbed his cowboy hat and fanned his face.

Mimi nodded, a tiny smear of sauce on her chin.

"I liked seeing the rainbow over the falls and getting wet from the mist. That was awesome!" Grant said.

"So, Mimi," Grant continued, "what makes the Great Lakes so great?"

"Well, where do I start?" Mimi said. "One of the main things you should know is that the Great Lakes hold about 20 percent of the fresh surface water in the world!"

"What's fresh water?" Grant asked. "It must not be the water at my school's water fountain, because it tastes old!"

Mimi laughed. "No, Grant," she said. "Fresh water is water on the earth that is not sea water from the ocean. It's found in lakes, rivers, streams...places like that. It's very important for the survival of people and animals on the earth."

DING! A text message arrived on Mimi's cell phone. "I wonder who that could be?" she said, and peered at her bright red phone.

"Oh, it's Ichabod, the lighthouse keeper!" Mimi read the message. She frowned. "Hmm, he seems a bit worried about the lighthouse. Something about odd noises in the night. Not like him. I hope he's okay. He's getting older. I'm not sure how much longer he can traipse up and down those lighthouse steps."

Christina and Grant stopped eating. They focused on Mimi.

Mimi snapped her phone shut. "Well, we're set to go see him. He can't wait!" she said with a smile.

Grant elbowed Christina. She leaned in and he whispered, "*Ichabod*. That's a creepy name. Sort of like that Headless Horseman dude?"

"Sure is creepy," Christina agreed.

Grant shook his head bouncing his blonde curls all around. "Sounds almost ...*icky*," he said, scrunching his face.

Christina nodded. "And what about him hearing odd noises? I'm not sure I want to meet Mr. Ichabod after all. Or visit his haunted lighthouse."

Christina hadn't really wanted to go on this trip to the Great Lakes with Mimi and Papa. Even though the fall leaves were spectacular hues of red, yellow, and orange, Christina wished they'd come in the summer so she could swim. Not in the fall, when it was too cold to go in the water, at least not on purpose! Now with the idea of spending time with a creepy lighthouse keeper, Christina wanted nothing more to do with the Great Lakes, and they'd hardly begun their journey.

Papa paid the bill and they left the restaurant. Soon, they were aboard the *Mystery Girl*.

"Where are we going now?" Grant asked.

"To Cleveland, Ohio, and Lake Erie," Papa replied.

"And the Rock and Roll Hall of Fame!" Christina added. She was a true rock and roll music lover. She couldn't wait to see all the guitars on display.

"So, we're not going to see Mr. Icky?" Grant asked.

Papa laughed. "Do you mean Mr. Ichabod?"

"Oops, yeah, Mr. Ichabod. Sorry, Papa," Grant said.

"We'll see him later in the trip, Grant," Mimi said.

"Let's get this plane up in the air! Let's rock and roll!" Papa cried, and the *Mystery Girl* launched into the crisp, bright blue autumn sky.

Grant played air guitar in his seat, bounding from side to side. At the end of his animated guitar solo, Grant shouted in his best Elvis Presley impersonation, "Thank you! Thank you very much!"

He bowed to the pretend crowd that had come to hear him play, flinging his arms to the side. WHACK! He accidentally hit Christina's shoulder.

"Ouch! Quit it, Grant!" Christina cried.

DING! DING! A text message suddenly appeared on Christina's cell phone. *Who could that be from*, she thought. Her eyes grew wide when she opened her phone to read it.

The text message said,

BEWARE OF BESSIE, THE EERIE MONSTER!

Christina immediately nudged Grant. "Look at this!" she whispered.

"Who is that from?" Grant asked.

Christina looked a second time at the message. There was no signature.

"I don't know," she replied and shrugged. "It doesn't say. Let me see what phone number sent it." Christina checked the number. Her mouth dropped open. "There isn't one!"

Goose bumps rose on Grant's arm. His big blue eyes grew wide with concern. "Maybe it's the Erie monster?"

Christina felt a chill, and pulled her sweater around her. "I sure hope not, because that's exactly where we're headed!"

2

TOO EERIE

Papa landed the *Mystery Girl* just outside Cleveland, Ohio, on a small airstrip.

As Papa taxied the plane to the red brick terminal building, Grant peered outside. "Hey, there's Papa's SUV," he remarked.

"And she's got the *Mystery Girl* boat *Mimi* hooked up behind her and ready to go with us," Papa said.

"Are we actually going to go boating on the lakes?" Christina asked. "I thought they were big and rough, even dangerous, this time of year."

"Of course, we are!" Mimi said. "There's a lot to see on the waters of the Great Lakes, like lighthouses, sunken ships, and islands," Mimi said. "The weather is supposed to be nice and the seas calm."

"Okay, everyone into the SUV and we're off to the hotel," Papa said.

"But I thought we were going to the see the Rock and Roll Hall of Fame!" Christina moaned.

"We are, but in the morning," Mimi replied, rummaging around in her floppy purse for some red lipstick.

Papa looked at his watch. "And judging from the time, we'd better get a move on if we want to get to our hotel before dark."

Grant and Christina piled into the back of Papa's big grey SUV. Mimi stepped up onto the sideboard of the truck in her spiky red heels and joined Papa in the front seat.

Christina didn't want to spend the night in a hotel. She wanted to go see all the interesting things in the Rock and Roll Hall of Fame. She knew there would be guitars and wild and crazy clothes that the stars had worn. But most of all, Christina wanted to hear some music, specifically from her favorite bands, which were, well, ALL OF THEM!